Good Night,
Little Kitten

Good Night, Little Kitten

Written by Nancy Christensen

Illustrated by Dennis Hockerman

My First READER

children's press®

A Division of Scholastic Inc.

New York Toronto London Auckland Sydney
Mexico City New Delhi Hong Kong
Danbury, Connecticut

Library of Congress Cataloging-in-Publication Data

Christensen, Nancy.
  Good night, little kitten / written by Nancy Christensen ; illustrated
by Dennis Hockerman.– 1st American ed.
        p. cm. – (My first reader)
Summary: A reluctant little kitten resists his parents' attempts to get
him to go to bed.
  ISBN 0-516-22926-5 (lib. bdg)   0-516-24628-3 (pbk.)
  [1. Bedtime–Fiction. 2. Cats–Fiction.] I. Hockerman, Dennis, ill.
  II. Title. III. Series.
  PZ7.C45264Go 2003
  [E]–dc21
                              2003003734

Note to Parents and Teachers

Once a reader can recognize and identify the 24 words
used to tell this story, he or she will be able to read successfully
the entire book. These 24 words are repeated throughout the story,
so that young readers will be able to easily recognize
the words and understand their meaning.

The 24 words used in this book are:

and	it's	said
bed	kitten	sleep
but	little	stay
don't	mama	time
for	must	to
go	night	up
good	now	want
I	papa	you

"Good night, Little Kitten,"

said Mama.

"I don't want to go to sleep,"

said Little Kitten.

"You must go to sleep,"

said Mama.

"I want to stay up,"

said Little Kitten.

"Good night, Little Kitten,"

said Papa.

"But I don't want to go

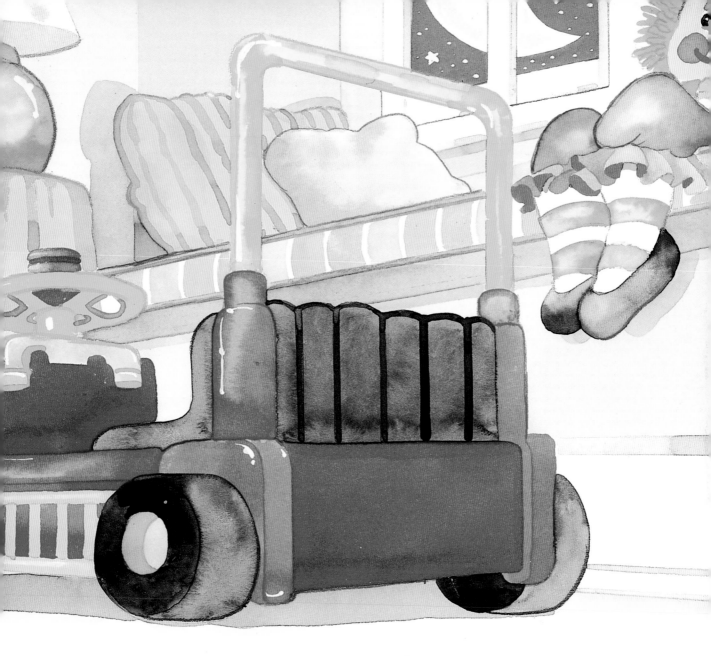

to sleep," said Little Kitten.

"It's time for bed,"

said Papa.

"I want to stay up,"

said Little Kitten.

"Go to sleep now!"

said Mama and Papa.

"Little Kitten?"

"Little Kitten?"

"Good night, Little Kitten!"